WRITTEN BY
STEPHANIE COOKE

ART BY
MARI COSTA

ETCH
HOUGHTON MIFFLIN HARCOURT
BOSTON NEW YORK

ETCH IS AN IMPRINT OF HOUGHTON MIFFLIN HARCOURT PUBLISHING COMPANY.

HMHBOOKS.COM

THE ILLUSTRATIONS IN THIS BOOK WERE DONE DIGITALLY IN CLIP STUDIO PAINT.
THE TEXT WAS SET IN WILDWORDS.
FLATTING BY REBECCA McCONNELL
COVER AND INTERIOR DESIGN BY MARY CLAIRE CRUZ
EDITED BY LILY KESSINGER

LIBRARY OF CONGRESS CATALOGING-IN-PUBLICATION DATA
NAMES: COOKE, STEPHANIE, 1986- AUTHOR.
TITLE: PARANORTHERN / STEPHANIE COOKE.
DESCRIPTION: BOSTON : HOUGHTON MIFFLIN HARCOURT, 2021. • AUDIENCE: AGES 10 TO 12. • AUDIENCE: GRADES 4–6. • SUMMARY: "IN THIS MIDDLE-GRADE GRAPHIC NOVEL, A WITCH NAMED ABBY AND HER THREE FRIENDS—A WOLF-GIRL, A GHOST, AND A PUMPKINHEAD—BAND TOGETHER TO TRY AND SAVE THEIR SUPERNATURAL TOWN FROM AN INVASION OF RABID (BUT ADORABLE) CHAOS BUNNIES." –PROVIDED BY PUBLISHER.
IDENTIFIERS: LCCN 2019044222 (PRINT) • LCCN 2019044223 (EBOOK) • ISBN 9780358168997 (HARDCOVER) • ISBN 9780358169000 (PAPERBACK) • ISBN 9780358164586 (EBOOK)
SUBJECTS: LCSH: GRAPHIC NOVELS. • CYAC: GRAPHIC NOVELS. • SUPERNATURAL–FICTION.
CLASSIFICATION: LCC PZ7.7.C6664 PAR 2021 (PRINT) • LCC PZ7.7.C6664 (EBOOK) • DDC 741.5/973–DC23
LC RECORD AVAILABLE AT HTTPS://LCCN.LOC.GOV/2019044222
LC EBOOK RECORD AVAILABLE AT HTTPS://LCCN.LOC.GOV/2019044223

MANUFACTURED IN CHINA
SCP 10 9 8 7 6 5 4 3 2 1
4500820951

WITCH'S BREW

...AN EXTRA-HOT LATTE WITH AN EXTRA SHOT OF ESPRESSO, NONFAT MILK, NO FOAM, AND–
–A SHOT OF LUCK FOR MY MEETING TODAY AT WORK, PLEASE.
AW, YOU DON'T NEED LUCK, MR. CHANEY!
UP NEXT, MOM, A–
I HEARD! COMIN' RIGHT UP.
CAN YOU POP OUT TO THE FRIDGE AND GET SOME MORE NONFAT MILK?
NO PROBLEM. KEVIN CAN TAKE OVER FOR A MINUTE.
I'LL BE BACK IN A SECOND.

–LEAVE ME ALONE!
PLEASE!
OR YOU'LL DO WHAT?

HEY! WHO'S BACK THERE?
DID YOU HEAR SOMETHING?
LET'S GET OUT OF HERE!

NYOOM
UGH...
I HATE BULLIES.
HELLO...?
sniff
sniff...
THOSE GUYS ARE GONE NOW.

ELLA!
ARE YOU OKAY?!
IT'S COOL IF YOU DON'T WANT TO TALK.
I JUST WANT TO MAKE SURE YOU'RE OKAY, THOUGH...
SNIFF
SNIFF

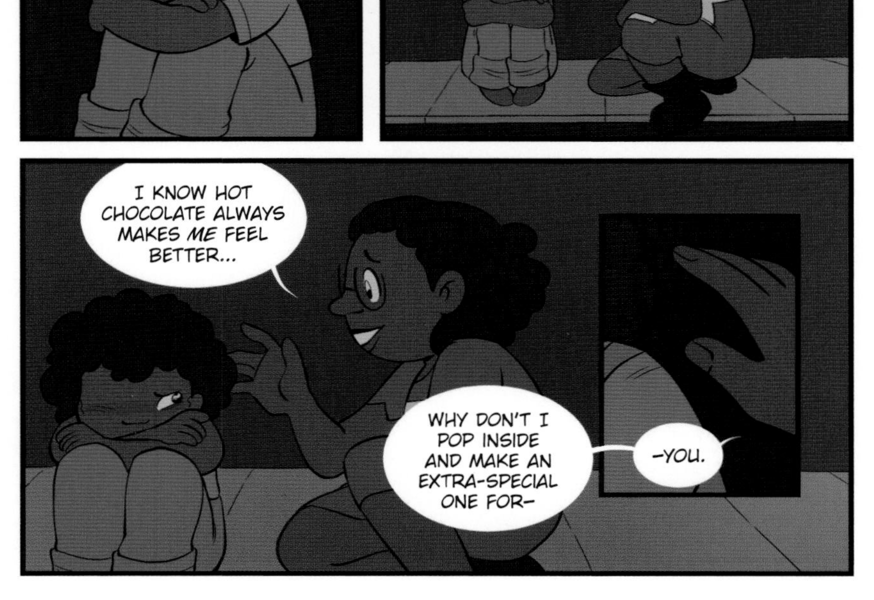
I KNOW HOT CHOCOLATE ALWAYS MAKES *ME* FEEL BETTER...
WHY DON'T I POP INSIDE AND MAKE AN EXTRA-SPECIAL ONE FOR–
–YOU.

ELLA, I JUST WANT TO HELP—
I DON'T **NEED** YOUR HELP!
ELLA—
Bzzt
WHOOSH!!

OOF...
THUD!
ELLA, WAIT!
HUH, THAT'S WEIRD...

WHERE HAVE YOU BEEN?
ARE YOU OKAY?
I THOUGHT YOU GOT LOCKED IN THE FRIDGE OR SOMETHING.
AND YOU DIDN'T THINK TO COME CHECK?
PFFT, IT'S BUSY IN HERE.
AND I KNEW YOU'D FIGURE IT OUT.
THANKS FOR THE CONCERN, MOM.
WHAT?! ISN'T IT BETTER THAT I BELIEVE IN YOUR ABILITIES?
NICE TRY.
HEY, KEV, I CAN TAKE OVER AGAIN. THANKS.
NO PROB, ABS.

WE SHOULD THINK ABOUT PUTTING A MAGIC MIRROR SURVEILLANCE SPELL IN THE ALLEY.
WHY WOULD WE DO THAT?
SOME SPEED DEMON KIDS WERE PICKING ON, UH, SOMEONE BACK THERE...
ARE THEY OKAY?
I THINK SO, BUT THEY RAN OFF PRETTY QUICK. I THINK THEY WERE EMBARRASSED.
KIDS CAN BE SO CRUEL.
I HOPE WHOEVER IT WAS GETS HOME ALL RIGHT.
ME TOO.

CAN I GET A PUMPKIN SPICE LATTE?
UGHHHHHHHHHHHHHHHHHHHHHHH
ISN'T THAT JUST TYPICAL!
SILAS!
WE'VE TALKED ABOUT THIS.
PUMPKIN SPICE LATTES ARE NOT MADE WITH ACTUAL PUMPKINS!
DO I GO AROUND OFFERING WITCH SMOOTHIES?
IT'S BARBARIC, ABBY.
BARBARIC!

PLEASE IGNORE MY FRIEND.
SORRY ABOUT HIM.
PLEASE TAKE A GREAT-DAY POTION ON THE HOUSE!
WHAT WAS *THAT*? I'M GOING TO BAN YOU *AGAIN* IF YOU KEEP SCARING AWAY CUSTOMERS.
I'M JUST HELPING THEM MAKE INFORMED CHOICES! IS THAT SO WRONG?!
WHEN IT MESSES WITH MY MOM'S BUSINESS THAT SHE BUILT FROM THE GROUND UP?
YES.
SORRY, MS. MORGAN...
YOU'RE PASSIONATE AND SMART. THAT'S GOING TO TAKE YOU PLACES SOMEDAY.
DON'T BE SORRY FOR THAT!
MOM!
DON'T ENCOURAGE HIM!
I'M GOING TO SIT DOWN WITH GITA AND HANNAH.
YOU'RE NOT EVEN ORDERING ANYTHING AFTER ALL THAT?!
NAH.

LATER...
CLOSED

MOOOOOOM?
I'M HUUUUNGRY!
I CAN FINISH UP HERE. GO CHECK ON ELLA.
YOU'RE THE BEST.
WE'LL HELP ABBY FINISH CLOSING UP!
DON'T WORRY, MS. MORGAN!
WHAT SHE MEANS IS *WE'LL* HELP. HANNAH FORGOT HER CORPOREAL CHARM *AGAIN*, SO SHE CAN'T TOUCH ANYTHING.
I'LL HELP SUPERVISE AND BE HERE FOR MORAL SUPPORT!
HOW CONVENIENT...

YOU FORGOT YOUR CHARM?!
SORRY!
HMMMM...
I CAN DO A QUICK SUMMONING SPELL FOR YOU!
THAT WOULD BE GREAT!
UMMON-SI, CORPOREAL CHARM!
I DON'T UNDERSTAND... THAT SHOULD'VE WORKED.
IT'S OKAY, ABS! I'LL JUST CHEER YOU ALL ON.
MY MAGIC HAS BEEN ACTING UP LATELY...
BLERGH.

THIS MIGHT BE A FOOLISH QUESTION, BUT WHY DO YOU NEED A CORPOREAL CHARM?
I'VE ONLY READ ABOUT THEM A BIT IN SCHOOL, BUT I DON'T REALLY GET IT.
SOME PEOPLE THINK GHOSTS ARE DEAD, BUT THAT'S JUST SILLY.
GHOSTS ARE BEINGS FROM OTHER DIMENSIONS THAT HAVE MOVED INTO A NEW WORLD.
DIFFERENT DIMENSIONS AFFECT BEINGS IN DIFFERENT WAYS.
WHEN I'M IN *THIS* DIMENSION, I LOSE MY CORPOREAL FORM IF I'M NOT WEARING MY CHARM, BUT IN MY HOME DIMENSION, I'M JUST NORMAL.
NO CORPOREAL CHARM NEEDED.
IN *THIS* DIMENSION, WE CAN'T PROPERLY INTERACT WITH OBJECTS ON OUR OWN.
WITHOUT A CORPOREAL CHARM, WE CAN'T PHYSICALLY TOUCH ANYTHING HERE, AND WE JUST MOVE THROUGH ALL

WHEN MY FAMILY IMMIGRATED HERE YEARS AGO, WE WERE ASSIGNED CORPOREAL CHARMS TO HELP TETHER US HERE.
THE GOVERNMENT ISSUES THEM TO KEEP INTERDIMENSIONAL TRAVEL AND IMMIGRATION CONTROLLED.
WHOAAAA, I HAD *NO IDEA!*
SO LIKE, CAN YOU WALK THROUGH WALLS AND STUFF WITHOUT YOUR CHARM THING?
THAT IS *SO COOL!*

WE'VE GOT THIS FROM HERE, KEV!
OKAY! THANKS, ABBY.
THANKS FOR ALL YOUR HELP TODAY.
SEE YA LATER!
YOU DON'T THINK WE SHOULD'VE ASKED HIM TO PLAY GAMES WITH US, RIGHT?
OPEN
I THINK HE *LIKES* YOU, ABBY!
HANN-AHHH, DON'T MAKE IT WEIRD.
I HAVE TO SEE HIM ALL THE TIME!
JUST CALLIN' IT LIKE I SEE IT.

OH, THAT'S A *REALLY* GOOD CARD. PLAY THAT ONE!
STOP CHEATING, HANNAH.
IT'S NOT CHEATING! I'M *HELPING*.
JUST LIKE YOU'RE HELPING ABBY CLEAN?
EXACTLY!
ALMOST DONE.
I JUST NEED TO TAKE THE GARBAGE OUT.
WE CAN HELP WITH THAT!

GREAT WORK, EVERYONE. KEEP IT UP!
GITA!

DID YOU *EAT* THAT BUNNY?!
NO!
...SOMETIMES MY ANIMAL SIDE JUST EMBRACES THE CHASE, YOU KNOW?
I MEAN, NO, NOT REALLY. I'M A VEGETARIAN.
MY MOM SAYS IT'S PART OF MATURING INTO WOLF ADOLESCENCE AND THAT I'LL BE ABLE TO CONTROL THE URGES SOON...
LET'S GET THIS GARBAGE IN THE BIN!
WE'VE GOT GAMES TO PLAY!

THE FUR TICKLES!
TWO BUNNIES IN THE ALLEY AT NIGHT?
WHERE DO YOU THINK THEY'RE COMING FROM?
MAYBE THERE'S A NEST NEARBY?
THEY BOTH CAME FROM DOWN THERE.
MAYBE WE SHOULD CHECK IT OUT...

TH—THUMP

WHAT IS IT, ABS?

UH, WELL, IT'S GOING TO SOUND WEIRD,

BUT IT FEELS LIKE SOMETHING IS PULLING ME DOWN THE ALLEY. IT'S LIKE A TUG...

I FEEL... *SOMETHING THERE...*

MAYBE WE SHOULDN'T GO FARTHER, THEN...

NO, NO, I'M TOTALLY OKAY.

LET'S GO.

Hop
Hop
Hop

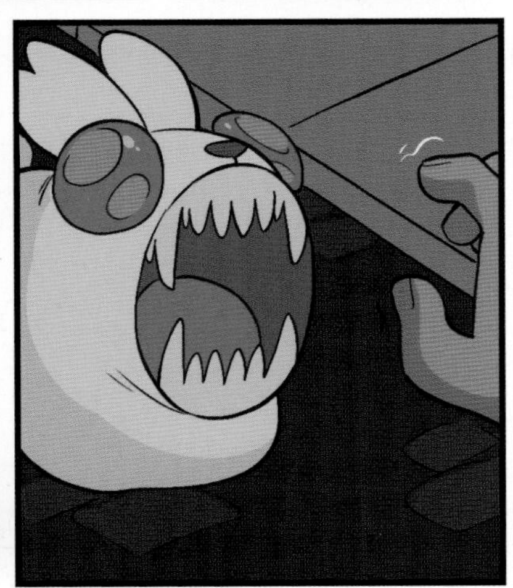

AAAAAA
CATCH!
SILAS!

HOW-
IS-
THIS-
BUNNY-
SO-
STRONG?
PULL
AHHHH!
WHAT DO I DO WITH IT NOW?!

QUICK!
PUT IT IN HERE!

THANKS, GITA.
IT WAS NOTHING...
THUNK
THUNK
THUNK
BRB, GUYS!

ELLA USED TO HAVE A JACKALOPE, AND WE KEPT THE CAGE!
YOU'RE GOING TO... KEEP IT?
WHAT ELSE ARE WE SUPPOSED TO DO WITH IT?
WHAT IF IT'S RABID?
CAN YOU ALL HELP ME GET IT IN HERE?

WHAT'S THAT LIGHT?
I'LL GET YOU SOME CARROTS TO NIBBLE ON LATER!

SORRY TO ASK THE OBVIOUS THING HERE, BUT IS *THAT* A PORTAL?!
YEP.
ARE THOSE ALL... BUNNIES?!
YEP.
WHAT KIND OF DIMENSION JUST HAS A BUNCH OF AGGRESSIVE *BUNNIES* IN IT?!
I DUNNO.
SO WHAT DO WE DO?
Boom!

HOW MANY BUNNIES DO YOU S'POSE ARE IN THERE?
SO MANY BUNNIES...
OH MY GOSH...

WE SHOULD GET SOMEONE TO HELP CLOSE THE PORTAL.
NO!
ABBY...
I'VE BEEN PRACTICING MY MAGIC A LOT LATELY.
IT'S BEEN GETTING STRONGER! BUT...
BUT WHAT?
...IT'S BEEN A LITTLE...
...UNPREDICTABLE...
ABS, *WHAT'S* GOING ON?
I DIDN'T MEAN TO DO IT.
DIDN'T MEAN TO DO *WHAT*?

I THINK I MIGHT'VE...
...MAYBE POSSIBLY...
...OPENED THE PORTAL...
YOU DID *WHAT?!*
WHAT WERE YOU THINKING?!
I DIDN'T MEAN TO!
EARLIER IN THE ALLEY, SOMETHING WEIRD HAPPENED...
WEIRD *HOW?*
WEIRD LIKE THERE WERE SOME KIDS PICKING ON ELLA.
YOUR SISTER, ELLA?
YEAH. SHE SEEMED UPSET, AND WHEN I WENT TO TRY TO HELP HER, MY MAGIC MUST'VE REACTED TO HER SOMEHOW.
THERE WAS LIKE, THIS SPARK, AND A BLAST OF ENERGY.
I THOUGHT IT WAS JUST A FLUKE...
MY HANDS WERE GLOWING AFTER, BUT THEN NOTHING HAPPENED.
WE REALLY SHOULD CALL SOMEONE TO HELP...
I OPENED THE PORTAL.
I-I'M PRETTY SURE I CAN CLOSE IT.

PRETTY SURE?
I CAN DO THIS.
AND *HOW* ARE *WE* GOING TO CLOSE THE PORTAL?
I HAVEN'T FIGURED THAT PART OUT YET...
B-BUT I WILL!
...
PLEASE— JUST LET ME TRY.
THERE ARE A *LOT* OF BUNNIES IN THERE.
I LOST COUNT! WHAT DID I MISS?
ABBY'S GOING TO TRY TO CLOSE THE PORTAL.
PORTALS CAN ONLY BE OPENED AND CLOSED BY *AUTHORIZED* MAGIC USERS AT THE CHMA.* THEY CAN BE *VERY* UNSTABLE IF NOT OPENED PROPERLY!
IT TAKES AN INCREDIBLY POWERFUL AND CONTROLLED AMOUNT OF MAGIC TO OPEN A PORTAL.
UNAUTHORIZED PORTALS CAN UPSET THE BALANCE OF THE *WHOLE* WORLD AND LET IN INVASIVE SPECIES FROM OTHER DIMENSIONS!
*CHMA: CENTRAL HAVEN MAGIC AUTHORITY

ABBY THINKS SHE MAY HAVE ACCIDENTALLY OPENED THE PORTAL.
THAT EXPLAINS WHY THE PORTAL *SMELLS* LIKE ABBY...
WHAT?!
ABBY, HOW?!
THAT MAGIC IS *WAY* TOO ADVANCED.
I DON'T KNOW...
BUT I'M GOING TO FIND A WAY TO CLOSE IT.
ABBY, YOU CAN GET IN A *LOT* OF TROUBLE FOR OPENING THIS PORTAL!
I DIDN'T MEAN TO...
MY MOM WORKS SO HARD TO TAKE CARE OF ELLA AND ME...
I *CAN'T* GET IN TROUBLE AND RISK NOT BEING HERE TO HELP THEM.
I *NEED* TO FIND A WAY TO CLOSE THIS PORTAL.
WELL... IF YOU OPENED IT, I KNOW YOU CAN CLOSE IT.
AND IT *IS* FAR EASIER FOR THE PERSON WHO OPENED THE PORTAL TO CLOSE IT.
PLUS, YOU HAVE *US* TO HELP YOU!
HA HA, WHOOPS!
CAN- YOU- GIVE- ME- A- HAND- WITH- THIS...

WHAT DO YOU NEED?

IF WE CAN GET THIS IN FRONT OF THE PORTAL, WE CAN STOP MORE BUNNIES FROM COMING THROUGH UNTIL ABBY CAN FIGURE OUT HOW TO CLOSE IT.

THAT'S A *GREAT* IDEA, GITA!
YOU'RE SO SMART.
I MEAN... IT'S ONLY REALLY A TEMPORARY FIX...

BUT IT'S AN *AMAZING* TEMPORARY FIX.

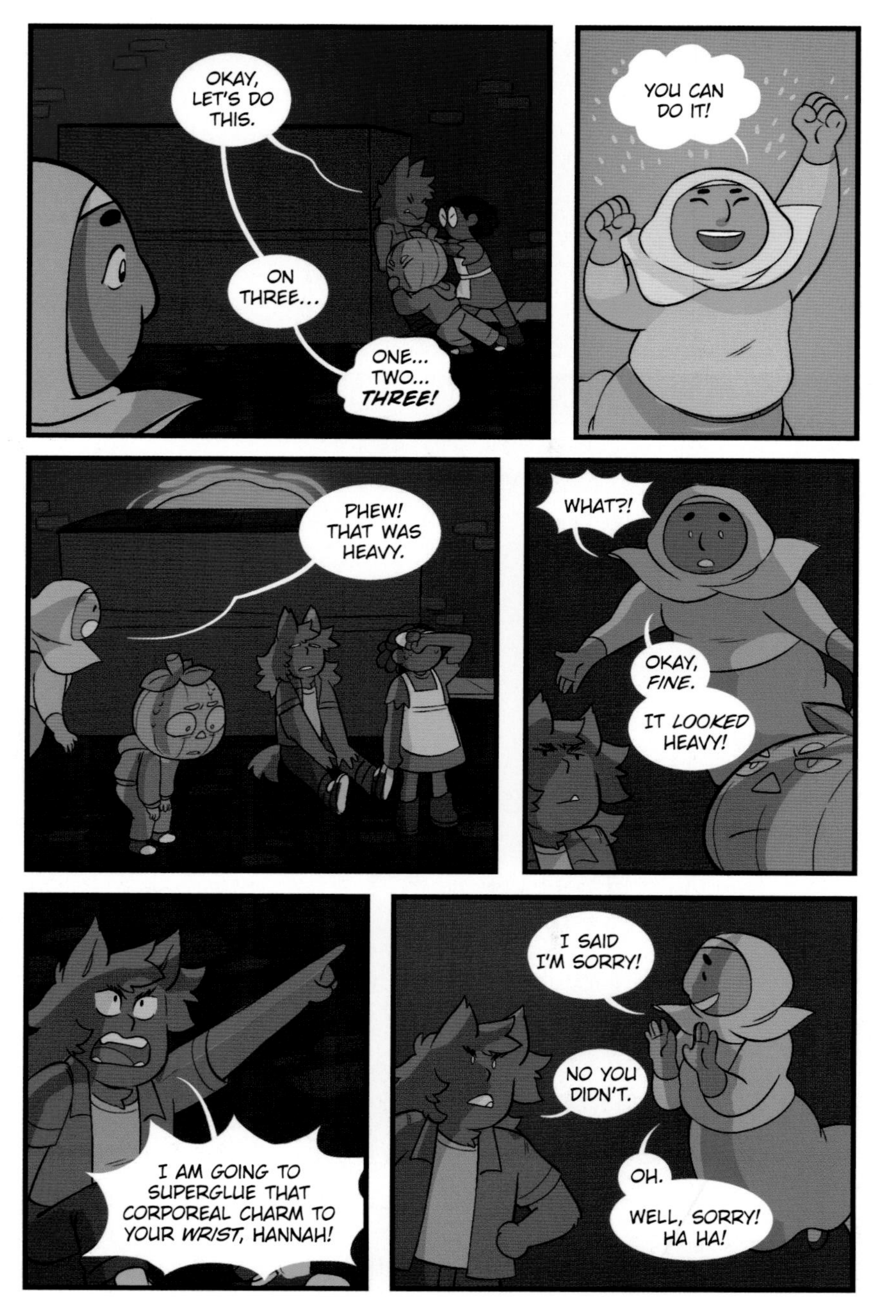
OKAY, LET'S DO THIS.
ON THREE...
ONE... TWO... *THREE!*
YOU CAN DO IT!
PHEW! THAT WAS HEAVY.
WHAT?!
OKAY, *FINE.*
IT *LOOKED* HEAVY!
I AM GOING TO SUPERGLUE THAT CORPOREAL CHARM TO YOUR *WRIST*, HANNAH!
I SAID I'M SORRY!
NO YOU DIDN'T.
OH.
WELL, SORRY! HA HA!

SO WHAT'S THE PLAN?
I HAVE TO DO SOME RESEARCH...
WE CAN GET IN A LOT OF TROUBLE IF WE DON'T CLOSE THIS PORTAL.
I HOPE YOU'RE RIGHT...
I CAN DO THIS, SILAS. I PROMISE.
BE BACK IN A SEC...
OH!
YOU GUYS!
I FOUND MY CORPOREAL CHARM!
IT WAS INSIDE THE *WHOLE TIME!*
HANNAH!

THUMP
THUMP
THUMP
THUMP

THE FOLLOWING MORNING...
Witch
6:15
shff
shff
RRRRRRRRRRR

I GUESS YOU'RE NOT A MORNING BUNNY.
MY SISTER, ELLA, DOESN'T LIKE MORNINGS EITHER.
LET'S GET OUT MY BESTIARY AND FIND OUT WHAT KIND OF BUNNY YOU ARE.
AND THEN WE'LL DO SOME READING UP ON PORTALS.
UNLESS YOU'RE A *TALKING* BUNNY AND YOU WANT TO SIMPLY *TELL ME* WHERE YOU CAME FROM!
OF COURSE...
HOW COULD IT POSSIBLY BE *THAT* EASY?

GRR
GRR
The Witch's Bestiary
The Witch's Bestiary
INDEX
INDEX
a
b
c

CHAOS BUNNY

THE ***ORYCTOLAGUS CHAOCULUS*** is a pesky member of the Leporidae family of the order Lagomorph. Most often referred to by its common name, the Chaos Bunny, it resides in a mammalia chaos realm, where it remains mostly harmless.

When in contact with anything outside its natural realm, its instincts are to immediately cause as much destruction and, well, chaos as possible.

While summoning this fluffy beast may *seem* relatively harmless, you should avoid the Chaos Bunny at **all costs!**

HMM... A CHAOS BUNNY, EH?
WHAT ARE WE GOING TO DO WITH YOU...?
AAAAAAAAAAAAAAAABBYYYY!
TIME TO MAKE SOME BREAKFAST.
I'LL FIND YOU A CARROT.
GRR
ABBY!
WHAT TOOK YOU *SO LONG*?
I'M STARVING TO ***DEAF!***
I THINK YOU MEAN *TO DEATH* UNLESS YOU'RE HAVING TROUBLE HEARING ME.
I CAN HEAR YOU, SILLY.
WHAT?
I SAID, *I CAN HEAR YOU!*
WHAT?
ABBY.

YOU FEELING BETTER TODAY?
MM-HMM!
WHAT DO YOU WANT FOR BREAKFAST, KIDDO?
PANCAKES!
PANCAKES IT IS!
COME ON, THEN...
...I NEED AN ASSISTANT TO TEST THE BATTER.
CAN WE PUT CHOCOLATE CHIPS IN THEM?!
ONLY IF *YOU* STIR THEM IN.
DEAL!

LATER...

PANCAKES FOR BREAKFAST?
UGH, YEP.
I'M STUFFED.
WELL, YOU'VE STILL GOT SOME ON YOUR FACE.
MO-OOOOOM, BOUNDARIES!

WHERE IS ELLA OFF TO?
SWADHI AND HER MOM PICKED HER UP FOR THEIR PLAYDATE.
I FORGOT THAT WAS TODAY.
WHAT'S THAT LOOK FOR?
WELL...
LET ME GUESS...
YOU NEED ME TO WORK?
I'M SORRY!
I WAS ASKED LAST MINUTE TO FILL IN OVER THE FALL BREAK FOR THE POTIONS TEACHER AT THE COLLEGE.
YEAH, NO PROBLEM, MOM.
I'M SORRY- YOU'RE A LIFESAVER!
I CAN'T WORK TOO LATE, THOUGH, OKAY?
I HAVE TO DO SOME STUDYING LATER.
STUDYING?
BUT YOU'RE OUT OF SCHOOL FOR THE FALL!
YOU SHOULD BE HAVING FUN AND GETTING INTO TROUBLE, AND UH, COVERING SHIFTS FOR YOUR FAVORITE AND ONLY MOTHER.
IT'S AN EXTRA-CREDIT PROJECT!
OH. WELL, GOOD.
GOOD FOR YOU! I'M PROUD OF YOU, ABS.
BUUUUUUUT... I GOTTA RUN.

HOW CAN I HELP YOU?
CAN I GET A MACCHIATO WITH AN EXTRA GOOD-DAY INFUSION?
SURE, NO-
-AND NO FOAM!
NO PROBLEM.

UHH...
BEWARE THE RABBITS OF CHAOS...
THAT COME TO US FROM AWAY.
POURING FORTH FROM THE PORTAL...
MORE AND MORE EVERY DAY.
THEIR HUNGER IS UNNATURAL...
...DESTROYING EVERYTHING IN ITS WAKE.
YOU MUST CLOSE THE PORTAL SOON...
OR THE RABBITS WILL MEAN OUR DOOM...

OH DEAR, DID I DO THAT?
IT'S OKAY. I'LL REMAKE IT.
WHAT HAPPENED? DID I GO INTO A TRANCE?
MY TRANCES CAN BE TERRIBLY PESKY SOMETIMES, ESPECIALLY SINCE THEY'RE USUALLY JUST ABOUT THE WEATHER...
RIGHT, YEAH, IT WAS ABOUT THE WEATHER.
IT'S GONNA RAIN LATER, APPARENTLY.
OH, ISN'T THAT FUNNY.
IT DOESN'T LOOK LIKE RAIN AT ALL!
HA! WELL, I'LL BELIEVE *YOU* OVER THE WEATHERMAN ANY DAY!
HOPEFULLY, I DON'T GET CAUGHT IN IT.
I'M NOT ALLOWED TO DRIVE WITH MY SPONTANEOUS TRANCING CONDITION.
THANKS FOR REMAKING MY DRINK, AND SORRY ABOUT THE MESS.
HAVE A NICE DAY!

ACROSS TOWN
RILEY RESIDENCE
GITA!
HAVE A SEAT. YOUR MOM AND I ARE JUST MAKING A LIGHT BREAKFAST.
LIGHT?
THIS IS LIGHT?
FOR YOU AND YOUR BROTHER?
SURE! YOU'RE GROWING WOLF PEOPLE, AND YOU NEED LOTS OF PROTEIN IN YOUR DIET.
WHEN I WAS YOUR AGE, I ATE TWICE AS MUCH FOR BREAKFAST...
DAD, STOP. HAVE YOU HEARD OF PORTION CONTROL?!
WE'RE TRYING TO HELP YOU, MY GITA.
LOOK AT YOUR BROTHER AND HOW MUCH HE EATS. IT'S GOOD FOR YOU.

BUT, MA, I'M NOT HUNGRY FOR THAT MUCH FOOD.
GITA, YOU ARE A GROWING GIRL WHO IS BECOMING A WOMAN.
YOU ALSO HAVE ANIMAL INSTINCTS THAT YOU NEED TO LEARN TO CONTROL.
THOSE INSTINCTS ARE GOING BANANAS WITH ALL THE HORMONAL CHANGES HAPPENING TO YOUR BODY.
THE PROTEIN WILL HELP YOU MAINTAIN YOUR SELF-CONTROL SO YOU DON'T DO ANYTHING ...UNTOWARD.
BUMP
AND, UH, THERE ARE OTHER URGES THAT COME WITH GROWING UP...URGES THAT INVOLVE ATTRACTION AND SE–
OKAY. NOPE!
NOPE, NOPE, NOPE... THIS CONVERSATION IS OVER.
IT IS TOO EARLY FOR THIS.
GITA–
I NEED TO GO FOR A RIDE.
I'LL BE BACK IN A BIT, MA.
BUT DON'T YOU WANT TO TALK ABOUT YOUR HORMONES MORE?!

THUD

GRRRR
WHAT THE-

THE SWAYZE HOME
AKA HANNAH'S HOUSE
...AND WHAT WAS DAD'S FAVORITE FOOD?
OOOOOH, MY BABA, YOUR DAD HAS GOT HOLLOW LEGS.
HANNAH'S ROOM
HE CAN EAT FOR DAYS!
HE NEARLY ATE US OUT OF HOUSE AND HOME, THAT ONE.
AND NOT A FUSSY EATER EITHER–HE ATE JUST ABOUT ANYTHING I PUT IN FRONT OF HIM...
...UH, WHAT DID YOU ASK, AGAIN?
WHAT WAS DAD'S FAVORITE–
OH, HIS FAVORITE FOOD! HIS FAVORITE WAS MY ROAST RUFKIN.
ROAST... RUFKIN?
WHAT'S A RUFKIN?

IT'S A VERY FLAVORFUL BIRD—
—I THINK I HAVE A PICTURE OF ONE ON MY CALENDAR...
THAT, MY BABA, IS A RUFKIN.
THAT'S JUST A CHICKEN!
ONE SEC, GRANDMA...
SEE, GRANDMA?
IT'S A CHICKEN!
BAH! THAT'S NO RUFKIN!
IT DOESN'T RESEMBLE A RUFKIN AT ALL.
WHAT DO THEY TEACH YOU IN THE SCHOOLS THERE...?

WHAT'S WRONG, BABA?
DID I SAY SOMETHING TO UPSET YOU?
...
BABA, I'M NOT A TELEPATH. YOU NEED TO TALK TO ME.
IT'S NOTHING, GRANDMA...
IT DOESN'T *SEEM* LIKE NOTHING.
DO YOU EVER FEEL LIKE YOU DON'T BELONG?
VERY MUCH.
I IMMIGRATED TO OUR HOME WHEN I WAS YOUNG TOO, AND-
I KNOW, I KNOW!
BUT *YOU* DIDN'T HAVE TO MOVE TO AN ENTIRELY NEW DIMENSION!
WE *LITERALLY* DON'T BELONG HERE.
I NEED A CHARM TO-
-AND YET YOU ARE THERE ANYWAY.
YEAH, BUT-
THERE ARE MANY PEOPLE WHO ARRIVE WHERE THEY DON'T BELONG, BUT LIFE IS ABOUT FINDING YOUR WAY WHEN YOU'RE LOST.
THERE'S NO ONE LIKE ME HERE.
I HAVE NEWS FOR YOU, BABA...
WHAT?
THERE'S NO ONE LIKE YOU *HERE* EITHER.
YOU ARE ONE OF A KIND, MY GIRL.
THANKS, GRANDMA...

I LOVE-
GRANDMA?

UH-OH...

ELSEWHERE IN NORTH HAVEN

CONSIDER HAVING A
GOURD-FREE HOLIDAY SEASON.
VISIT TPS.NORTH.ORG FOR MORE
DETAILS AND TO SIGN OUR PETITION.
FROM CONCERNED MEMBERS
OF THE PUMPKINHEAD SOCIETY
(TPS)

WHAT'S THIS FOR?
I HOPE IT'S A PARTY!
WHAT IS IT?
IT'S A STUPID JOKE.
IT'S NOT A JOKE.
YOU CAN GO TO OUR WEBSITE TO FIND OUT MORE-
WE DON'T WANT TO FIND OUT MORE ABOUT YOUR SILLY PUMPKIN BOYCOTT.
CAN YOU BELIEVE HIM?
LET'S GO...

WHAT A LOSER.
LIKE, LEARN TO PICK YOUR BATTLES, DUDE.
TO-TAL-LY.
FWIP
...

THAT'S CASPARITA AND JARRAH'S BOY, RIGHT?
YEEEEP–
HE'S A WEIRD ONE, THAT BOY...

11:28
54%
Hannah
r u seein tis *this
Gita
u mean
Hannah
they took out the in my
Gita
they took out your lightning?
Hannah
POWER!!!!
Abby
oooooh every1 ok?
Hannah
ya
Gita
a bit banged up but ok
Hannah
gud. lets meet at in 20
Me
Yes
Abby
Gita
Me
send

WITCH'S BREW

RING
RING
HEYA!

UH, WHAT'S UP, GUYS?

HAVE YOU NOT BEEN OUTSIDE AT ALL?
NOT YET. I'VE BEEN HELPING OUT HERE ALL MORNING.
WHAT.
IS.
IT?
UH, WELL... THERE ARE–
–BUNNIES–
–EVERYWHERE!
WELL, I SAW THEM OUTSIDE MY HOUSE.
GITA AND SILAS BOTH SAW BUNNIES TOO, THOUGH.
BUNNIES LIKE THAT ONE THAT *ATTACKED* ME LAST NIGHT!

DID YOU CHECK ON THE PORTAL TODAY?
UMM...WELL, I MADE ELLA BREAKFAST FIRST THING THIS MORNING, AND THEN I CAME DOWN TO HELP OUT HERE.
WE KNOW YOU DO A LOT, ABS. IT'S OKAY.
YEAH, BUT SOMETHING REAL WEIRD IS GOING ON IN NORTH HAVEN.
SO MORE BUNNIES GOT OUT?
WE SHOULD GO CHECK THE DUMPSTER.
KEVIN, WE'LL BE BACK IN A BIT!

OH GOSH,
I GUESS THAT'S
NOT GOOD.

DID YOU FIND OUT ANYTHING ABOUT THE PORTAL?
HOW WE CAN CLOSE IT?
WEEEEEELL...
UH...
ABBY-
IT'S OKAY IF YOU NEED TO ASK FOR HELP.
I CAN DO IT!
I KNOW I CAN.
UMMON-SI, BESTIARY!
Thwip!
HA HA HA...
LET ME JUST GRAB THAT...

WHERE IS IT...?
WHERE IS IT...?
AHA!
I FOUND THIS EARLIER...
THAT'S WHAT THEY ARE?
YEAH— CHAOS BUNNIES.
FROM A DIMENSION OF, UH, WELL, CHAOS.
AAAAAAAAAA
POOF

AHHHHHHHH!
GET BACK, DEMON RABBIT!
AAAARGH

SO, LIKE, THE BUNNIES COME FROM THIS OTHER DIMENSION WHERE EVERYTHING IS JUST, UH, CHAOS?
YEAH, EXACTLY. I THINK...
AND THEY WANT TO CAUSE CHAOS *HERE* NOW TOO?
I THINK IT'S JUST IN THEIR NATURE TO DESTROY EVERYTHING AROUND THEM.
AT LEAST THEY LOOK REAL CUTE WHILE DOING IT!
WHAT?!
WHAT IF IT WAS A DIMENSION OF CHAOS TOADS OR SNAKES?
THAT WOULD BE *SUPER* ICKY!
BUT WE STILL HAVEN'T FIGURED OUT HOW TO CLOSE THE PORTAL–

ABBY...
OR HOW IT WAS EVEN POSSIBLE FOR ABBY TO OPEN IT TO BEGIN WITH! IT TAKES SOME *REALLY* POWERFUL MAGIC.
I, UHH...
I NEED SOME MORE TIME. TODAY JUST GOT AWAY FROM ME...
ABBY!
WE DON'T *HAVE* TIME. THE BUNNIES ARE ALREADY ALL OVER THE PLACE–
I, UHH...
FIND THE SOURCE, ABBY!
DID YOU GUYS HEAR–
–HEAR WHAT?

UH, NOTHING. NEVER MIND.
FIND THE SOURCE!
I-*WE*-NEED TO FIND THE SOURCE!
THE SOURCE OF WHAT?

RIGHT. UH, I MEAN-
THE SOURCE. OF YOUR MAGIC!
I MEAN, THE SOURCE OF MY MAGIC THAT OPENED THE PORTAL.

THE SOURCE?
YEAH! EXACTLY.
UH, SORRY, BUT I'M NOT FOLLOWING...
WELL...
THIS MAGIC IS *REALLY* ADVANCED FOR ME. WE HAVEN'T EVEN STUDIED PORTALS IN SCHOOL YET—
I LEARNED ALL ABOUT THEM ON MY OWN WHEN WE WERE MOVING HERE!
PORTALS ARE *SO* NEAT.
WELL,
I THINK MAYBE THIS HAS SOMETHING TO DO WITH MY MAGIC THAT'S BEEN ON THE FRITZ.

!
WHAT DID YOU SEE?
I DON'T KNOW, BUT IT WAS BIGGER THAN A BUNNY...

WHOEVER'S OVER THERE...
COME ON OUT.
ELLA!
WHAT ARE YOU *DOING* BACK HERE?!
YOU SHOULDN'T BE PLAYING IN THE ALLEY. YOU COULD'VE BEEN HURT, OR–
RAWR!

OOH, LOOK!

OHH NO— I'M NOT FALLING FOR *THAT.*
IT'S A FLUFFY BUNN-
THE CHAOS BUNNIES!

ABBY!
IT'S COMING TOWARD US REAL FAST!

STOP!

OH MY GOOOOOOSH!
ABBY!
ARE YOU OKAY?!
WHAT JUST HAPPENED...?
UH, WE WERE HOPING *YOU* COULD TELL *US*.
UGHHHHH...
SIT BACK DOWN— YOU'RE HURT!
I'M FINE. REALLY—

ABBY?
...
ABBY!
ABBY, PLEASE WAKE UP...

WHERE AM I...?

ABBY...
...ABBY...
ABBY!
Gasp!

WELCOME, ABBY.
UH, THANKS, I GUESS?
BUT, UMM, WHERE AM I?
WAIT–
AM I DEAD?!

I AM MORRIGAN.
THIS...
IS MY DOMAIN.
OOOOOOOOHH, RIGHT, GOTCHA...
YOUR DOMAIN.
AND WHERE IS "YOUR DOMAIN" EXACTLY?

BLOOD OF MY BLOOD, YOU HAVE BEEN BROUGHT HERE TO SEE.
TO SEE? SEE WHAT?
YOUR *TRUE* POTENTIAL!
MY TRUE POTENTIAL?
THERE IS POWER IN OUR BLOOD THAT IS PASSED DOWN THROUGH THE GENERATIONS...

POWER THAT IS YOUR BIRTHRIGHT...
CENTRAL HAVEN GRAND OPENING
BUT **BE WARNED:** THE PRICE OF POWER CAN BE STEEP...

MAGIC IS IN ALL OF US, BUT *POWER* CORRUPTS.
I HAVE *SO* MANY QUESTIONS...
I'M AFRAID TIME IS RUNNING OUT.
YOU MUST SOON RETURN TO YOUR WORLD.
BUT–
ABBY MORGAN, BLOOD OF MY BLOOD, YOU CAN DO GREAT THINGS.
LET OUR ANCESTRAL MAGIC GUIDE YOU, AND REMEMBER TO TRUST YOURSELF.
DO NOT LISTEN TO THE CORRUPTING WHISPERS OF THE POWER–IT WILL OFFER YOU A GREAT MANY THINGS, BUT THEY ARE *ALL* LIES THAT WILL LEAD YOU DOWN A DARK PATH.
HOW WILL I TELL THE VOICES APART?
YOU WILL KNOW.
TIME IS UP.
BUT–
WAKE!

GASP
ABBY!
UH, GITA?
I THINK YOU MIGHT BE KILLING ABBY A LITTLE BIT.
ARE YOU OKAY, ABBY?
WE WERE SO WORRIED ABOUT YOU!
YOU JUST... COLLAPSED!

I THINK I'M OKAY? I FEEL OKAY...
ALTHOUGH I MIGHT HAVE A COUPLE BRUISES...
WHAT HAPPENED?
I-I DON'T KNOW.
DO YOU *REMEMBER* WHAT HAPPENED BEFORE THIS?
TALK TO US.
WHAT'S THE LAST THING YOU REMEMBER?
WELL...
ELLA JUMPED OUT AT US FROM BEHIND THE DUMPSTER...
THEN-
-AND THEN I HAD A WEIRD DREAM...

SO YOU DON'T REMEMBER THE SPELL YOU CAST?
UHH... WHAT?
YOU WENT ALL-
AND THEN YOU WERE ALL-
AND *THEN* YOU WENT LIKE-
UH...
WELL...
I GUESS I DON'T REALLY REMEMBER ALL THAT.

SO I DID THAT TO THE CHAOS BUNNY?
YOU REALLY DON'T REMEMBER?
MAYBE WE SHOULD GET SOME HELP...
WE'RE LIKE–
–REALLY WORRIED ABOUT YOU, ABS!
I'M FINE!
I'M–
I'M FINE. REALLY.
I JUST NEED TO FIGURE OUT WHAT'S GOING ON WITH MY MAGIC.

THERE WAS A VOICE—BEFORE I BLACKED OUT. IT WAS TALKING TO ME, AND IT WAS LIKE SHE WAS TRYING TO HELP ME. I THOUGHT WE COULD *ALL* HEAR IT—SHE SOUNDED SO LOUD—
SHE?
YEAH, IT WAS A WOMAN. HER NAME WAS MORRIGAN.
WHEN I FAINTED, I DIDN'T KNOW WHAT WAS GOING ON. I WASN'T *HERE* ANYMORE. SHE CALLED WHEREVER WE WERE HER "DOMAIN." IT WAS LIKE A GOTH DREAM HOUSE. SHE TOLD ME THAT I HAVE POWER IN MY BLOOD.
THAT MAKES SENSE—YOU *ARE* A WITCH.
IT WAS *MORE* THAN THAT. SHE SAID IT WENT *BEYOND* WHAT I THOUGHT I COULD BE CAPABLE OF. IT KIND OF...WELL, IT KIND OF SCARED ME.

WE *WILL* FIGURE OUT HOW TO CLOSE THE PORTAL.
I'M GOING TO HUNKER DOWN AND DO SOME RESEARCH.
OKAY, ABBY...
I SENSE A "BUT" COMING. IS THERE A "BUT" COMING?
HEHEHE... BUTTS.
BUT...
KNEW IT...
BUT...
YOU NEED TO TALK TO US AND LET US KNOW IF THIS IS ALL TOO MUCH FOR YOU.
OKAY?
OKAY.
AAAAA

Pop!
!

NO!
THE CAFÉ!
WAAAH, GET IT OUT OF HERE!
THIS IS A HEALTH CODE VIOLAAAAATION!

SHOO!

AIYEEEEEE!

MOM IS GONNA FREAK!
WE SHOULD SPLIT UP AND TRY TO CATCH IT.
DON'T GO UNARMED-GRAB SOMETHING TO KEEP BETWEEN YOU.
GO STAND BY KEVIN-WE'VE GOT THIS!

SWING

click

click
SLAM!
BETTER KEEP *THAT* TIGHTLY SHUT.

OOF. THIS PLACE IS A MESS.

I BETTER GET THIS CLEANED UP BEFORE MY MOM SEES.
WHY DON'T I MEET UP WITH YOU LATER?
PFFT, AS IF WE'RE GOING TO MAKE YOU CLEAN THIS ALL UP BY YOURSELF.
WE'RE A TEAM!
YEAH!
AND I EVEN HAVE MY CHARM TODAY, SO I CAN HELP TOO.

LET'S SHUT IT DOWN EARLY, KEV.
I THINK IT'S GOING TO BE A QUIET NIGHT. YOU CAN HEAD OUT!

WHY DON'T YOU HEAD UPSTAIRS AND GET INTO YOUR PAJAMAS?
I'LL BE UP SOON AND WE CAN MAKE SOMETHING TO EAT.
OKEY-DOKEY!

DID YOU CLEAN THE CAFÉ TODAY?
IT LOOKS GOOD IN HERE...
MWAH
ELLA IS UPSTAIRS. WE WERE GOING TO MAKE SOME DINNER SHORTLY.
THAT SOUNDS GREAT– I'LL PUT MY STUFF AWAY AND JOIN YOU.
HAVE YOU ALL BEEN OUTSIDE TODAY? THERE WERE BUNNIES *EVERYWHERE!* MUST BE MATING SEASON OR SOMETHING...
HA HA HA, OR SOMETHING...
I'LL SEE YOU UPSTAIRS.

YAAAWN
I THINK WE SHOULD GET SOME REST.
I'M GOING TO MARATHON OLD EPISODES OF *CRYSTAL RIDERS* UNTIL I FALL ASLEEP...
YOU SHOULD WALK HOME TOGETHER.
I'M GOING TO HELP MAKE DINNER WITH MY MOM AND ELLA, AND THEN I HAVE TO DO SOME RESEARCH ON HOW WE'RE GOING TO CLOSE THIS PORTAL.
THAT'S GOOD, ABS. GIVE US A SHOUT IF YOU NEED HELP.
LET'S CHECK IN TO THE GROUP CHAT LATER, COOL?

WITCH'S BREW

SHUT

THE FOLLOWING MORNING...
HA HA HA...
WHOOPS!
YOU COULD ALWAYS JUST ASK WHAT I'M DOING.

OKAY, SMARTYPANTS! WHAT ARE YOU DOING, THEN?
A HISTORY OF WITCHCRAFT?
A History of Witchcraft
YOU DOING SOME READING FOR THAT EXTRA-CREDIT PROJECT?
OH, UH-YEAH!
I REALLY WANT TO GET AHEAD OF MY WORK FOR THE SCHOOL YEAR.
HEY, MOM? WHAT DO YOU KNOW ABOUT MORRIGAN?
MORRIGAN?
NOD

SIGH
SOME WEIRD STUFF HAS HAPPENED THIS WEEK...
WEIRD STUFF LIKE WHAT?
OKAY, SO THE LAST FEW WEEKS, MY MAGIC HAS BEEN SORT OF, LIKE...
...ON THE FRITZ...
SO YOU'RE NOT DOING AN EXTRA-CREDIT PROJECT FOR FALL BREAK, THEN?
NO...
I JUST DIDN'T WANT TO WORRY YOU. YOU'RE SO BUSY, AND–
I KNOW I'M BUSY AND TAKE ON A LOT, BUT YOU AND ELLA ARE MY *EVERYTHING.* YOU CAN COME TO ME WITH ANYTHING AND WE'LL TACKLE IT TOGETHER.
AS A FAMILY.
NOW, WHAT'S GOING ON?

MY MAGIC HAS BEEN ACTING STRANGE LATELY.
STRANGE HOW?
IT'S BEEN, LIKE, OUT OF SYNC WITH ME.
SPELLS NOT QUITE WORKING RIGHT...
AND I'VE BEEN ABLE TO CAST SPELLS THAT ARE *WAY* ADVANCED.
AND THEN YESTERDAY WE WERE IN THE ALLEY AND I HEARD A VOICE SPEAKING TO ME. IT WAS *SO WEIRD*, MOM. IT SOUNDED LIKE SHE WAS RIGHT BESIDE ME–
AND THEN SOMETHING STARTLED ME IN THE ALLEY AND I WENT INTO THIS TRANCE–
A TRANCE?!
YEAH, BUT I DON'T REMEMBER IT...
DON'T GIVE ME THAT LOOK!
SORRY! I'M JUST CONCERNED. I'LL TRY TO BE LESS OF A GOOD MOTHER.
I CAPTURED AND CONFINED A BUNNY IN A LEVITATION SPHERE.
I DIDN'T THINK YOU'D LEARNED THAT YET.
THAT'S THE THING! I *HAVEN'T* LEARNED IT YET. SOMETHING HAPPENED TO ME WHEN I WAS IN THE TRANCE AND IT, LIKE, CHANNELED POWERS THAT I DON'T HAVE!
AND WHAT DOES THIS ALL HAVE TO DO WITH MORRIGAN?

THE VOICE I HEARD...
SHE SAID HER NAME WAS MORRIGAN.
I'VE BEEN TRYING TO RESEARCH HER AND SOME OTHER THINGS ALL NIGHT.
HMM... MAYBE I CAN HELP A BIT.
The Three Ravens

I REMEMBER THIS BOOK-
YOU USED TO READ IT TO ME
WHEN I WAS LITTLE.
I DID. I THOUGHT I'D
GET AROUND TO TELLING YOU
THAT ALL MYTHS AND FOLKLORE ARE
BASED IN TRUTHS, AT LEAST IN PART.
THIS IS THE STORY OF YOUR
ANCESTOR, MORRIGAN.
MY...
ANCESTOR?!
WELL, *OUR*
ANCESTOR, I
SUPPOSE, BUT
YEAH.

BEFORE THE HAVENS WERE FULLY FORMED–WHEN WE ALL LIVED IN THE WILDS– COVENS CAME TO HER IN DROVES, BEGGING FOR AND TRYING TO BUY HER ALLEGIANCE.

ON HER JOURNEYS SHE MET DAGDA, A MAN WHO LED HIS COVEN LIKE A FATHER. HE CARED FOR AND LOVED EVERYONE IN HIS VILLAGE.
MORRIGAN SAW THIS AND FELL DEEPLY IN LOVE WITH HIM. SHE FINALLY SETTLED DOWN WITH HIM AND HIS PEOPLE.
THEY WERE VERY HAPPY, AND EVENTUALLY, THEY STARTED A FAMILY. MORRIGAN GAVE BIRTH TO TWIN GIRLS, BRIGIT AND MIDIR, AND SHE LOVED THEM DEARLY.
THE TWINS GREW UP, AND ON THE CUSP OF ADULTHOOD, A GREATER POWER THAN THEY HAD KNOWN BEGAN TO MANIFEST IN THEM.
MORRIGAN GUIDED THE YOUNG WOMEN AS BEST SHE COULD, BUT JUST AS WHEN SHE HERSELF HAD BEEN YOUNG, MANY COVENS CAME TO PRESENT OFFERINGS, THIS TIME TO HER DAUGHTERS.
BRIGIT WAS KIND AND COMPASSIONATE AND REFUSED THE GIFTS, CHOOSING TO CONTINUE HER STUDIES AND HELP THOSE IN NEED. MIDIR, HOWEVER, WAS SWAYED BY THE GIFTS.

SHE SAW THE POTENTIAL IN TAKING ADVANTAGE OF THESE PEOPLE AND HOW SHE COULD LIVE AN EASY LIFE AS THEY ALL FOUGHT FOR HER POWER.
SHE SENT THEM ON QUESTS TO AMUSE HERSELF, SET CHALLENGES TO SEE WHO WAS WORTHY OF HER ABILITIES.
BUT SOON SHE GREW BORED AND WISHED FOR THE STAKES TO BE HIGHER. SHE PITTED PEACEFUL COVENS AGAINST ONE ANOTHER, TELLING THEM THAT ONLY THE STRONGEST WOULD BE WORTHY.
MORRIGAN WATCHED IN HORROR AS MIDIR BROUGHT DESTRUCTION TO THE WORLD AROUND HER, CORRUPTED BY THE POWER AND ATTENTION.
THE POWER BEGAN TO CONSUME MIDIR, WITHERING HER BODY AND SOUL, BUT STILL SHE DID NOT STOP. IT BROKE MORRIGAN TO SEE HER DAUGHTER STRAY DOWN SUCH A DARK PATH, SO SHE DEVISED A PLAN.
SHE SET OUT TO VISIT HER DAUGHTER, WHO WAS LIVING IN A GRAND HOUSE THAT HAD BEEN CONSTRUCTED FOR HER.
IT WAS PACKED TO THE RAFTERS WITH GIFTS THAT HAD BEEN PRESENTED TO HER, AND SERVANTS FROM NEIGHBORING COVENS WHO CARRIED OUT HER EVERY WHIM.

UPON ENTERING THE HOUSE, MORRIGAN RUSHED TO HER DAUGHTER AND EMBRACED HER, TEARS STREAMING DOWN HER FACE.
AS SHE HELD MIDIR TIGHT TO HER CHEST, SHE WHISPERED A SPELL, AND SLOWLY MIDIR'S BODY BEGAN TO TRANSFORM.
MIDIR PULLED AWAY IN HORROR AND WATCHED AS SHE BEGAN TO GROW BLACK FEATHERS ALL OVER HER BODY.
MIDIR TRIED TO CRY OUT, BUT ALL THAT ESCAPED HER LIPS WAS A ***CAW.*** HER BODY SHRANK, AND SOON ALL THAT WAS LEFT OF MIDIR WAS A BEAUTIFUL BLACK RAVEN.
WHEN MORRIGAN RETURNED HOME WITH MIDIR, SHE PROMPTLY TOLD DAGDA AND BRIGIT WHAT HAD TRANSPIRED.
OVERCOME WITH GRIEF AT THE LOSS OF HER SISTER AND UNABLE TO IMAGINE A WORLD WITHOUT HER OTHER HALF, BRIGIT CAST THE SAME SPELL, TURNING HERSELF INTO A RAVEN.

MORRIGAN LOOKED TO DAGDA, HER HEART BROKEN, BUT DAGDA JUST WALKED TO HER CALMLY AND KISSED HER ON THE FOREHEAD, TELLING HER TO BE WITH HER DAUGHTERS.
MORRIGAN NODDED AND THE SPELL WAS CAST ONCE MORE, LEAVING BEHIND THREE RAVENS THE COLOR OF NIGHT.
UHHHH...
YOU SAW MORRIGAN AFTER THE TRANCE.
YEAH... I DID.
MY GRANDMOTHER USED TO TELL STORIES OF MORRIGAN. SHE TOLD US THAT MORRIGAN APPEARED TO THE STRONGEST WITCHES IN OUR FAMILY THROUGHOUT THE GENERATIONS.
HOW DID SHE APPEAR TO *ME*?
I DON'T KNOW, TO BE HONEST.
SOME FOLKS SAY THAT WHEN SHE TOOK THE FORM OF A RAVEN, IT EXTENDED HER LIFE AND SHE'S STILL HERE.
I PERSONALLY THINK SHE LIVES SOMEWHERE IN BETWEEN THIS WORLD AND THE NEXT. SHE LINGERS TO GUIDE THE WOMEN OF OUR FAMILY AND STEER THEM AWAY FROM THE PATH MIDIR TOOK.

MORRIGAN *WAS* INCREDIBLY POWERFUL, AND WHATEVER GAVE HER THOSE POWERS IS IN OUR BLOOD.
SO HOW DO I LEARN TO CHANNEL MY POWERS?
IF I *DON'T* LEARN, WILL I TURN INTO A RAVEN?!
WELL, I DON'T KNOW ABOUT THE RAVEN PART, BUT I *DO* KNOW THAT YOU ARE A GOOD GIRL. YOU ALWAYS HAVE BEEN.
DON'T LET THE POWER TEMPT YOU AND CORRUPT THAT.
I'VE ALWAYS WANTED TO HELP PEOPLE, LIKE MORRIGAN DID.
YOUR FATHER IS THE SAME WAY, BUT HE FELT HE WOULD THRIVE IN THE WILDS WITH THE RECLUSIVE COVENS, AND I KNEW I WANTED TO BE IN THE HAVENS AMONGST THE UNITED SUPERNATURALS.
I LEARNED TO MEDITATE SO I COULD BE IN TUNE WITH MY MIND AND BODY BETTER. IT HELPED—AND *STILL* HELPS—ME TO FEEL MY LIMITS.

I BELIEVE IN YOU, MY DARLING GIRL, BUT IF YOU STILL FEEL AFRAID, TALK TO HER AGAIN.
HOW AM I GOING TO DO THAT?!
TRY HOLDING A SÉANCE.
A SÉANCE? I THOUGHT THEY ONLY WORKED WITH THE DEAD.
I SAID I DON'T *KNOW* IF SHE'S DEAD. IT CAN'T HURT TO TRY, RIGHT?
I GUESS...
WHAT'S THE WORST THAT CAN HAPPEN? YOU ACCIDENTALLY SUMMON A DEMON? HA HA HA...
MOOOOOOM...
THE TRASH BIN IS GETTING SUPER FULL. I'M GOING TO QUICKLY TAKE IT OUT.
NOOOOO!!!
I, UH, JUST MEAN THAT YOU DESERVE A BREAK.
I'LL TAKE IT OUT.

LATER...
I THINK THAT'S EVERYTHING...
KNOCK KNOCK!
YOU KNOW YOU DON'T HAVE TO SAY "KNOCK KNOCK" WHEN THERE'S AN *ACTUAL* DOOR TO KNOCK ON, RIGHT?
WHAT'S ALL THIS?
WE'RE GOING TO HOLD A SÉANCE!
A SÉANCE? LIKE, TO TALK TO THE DEAD?
WELL, SORT OF. WE'RE GOING TO TALK TO AN ANCESTOR OF MINE.
WHAT'S THE "SORT OF," THEN?
I'M NOT SURE THAT SHE'S DEAD.
OH. OKAY, THEN.
GRRRRRR

HEY, ABS!
GITA! SILAS!
SILAS...?
YOU OKAY, SILAS?
UGH, I SAW THESE GIRLS FROM YESTERDAY DOWNSTAIRS... IT PUT ME IN A *MOOD.*
PLUS, THESE BUNNIES ARE *EVERYWHERE.* IT'S LIKE I'M CONSTANTLY LOOKING OVER MY SHOULDER TO MAKE SURE ONE ISN'T ABOUT TO ATTACK ME!
I'LL BE FINE, THOUGH... WE'LL GET THE PORTAL CLOSED SOON AND *EVERYTHING WILL BE FINE.*
SO WHAT'S THIS ABOUT HOLDING A SÉANCE?
YEAH! SO... UHHH...
I NEED TO COMMUNE WITH A SPIRIT...
...WHO MAY OR MAY NOT BE DEAD...
SO WE'RE GOING TO HOLD A SÉANCE!
DOES THIS HAVE ANYTHING TO DO WITH THE VOICE YOU HEARD?

YEAAAAAH...IT TURNS OUT THAT I WASN'T IMAGINING IT.
A REALLY POWERFUL ANCESTOR OF MINE WAS SPEAKING TO ME.
IF I CAN TALK TO HER AGAIN, I THINK SHE CAN HELP ME CHANNEL THE POWER I NEED TO CLOSE THE PORTAL.
CAN WE HELP SET UP?
NAH, YOU CAN JUST RELAX UNTIL WE START. I'M NOT SURE THIS SÉANCE IS EVEN GOING TO WORK...

LET'S GET STARTED!
IGHT-LI.
SNAP!
ARKNESS-DI!

WHAT'S ALL THE SAGE FOR?
SAGE HELPS TO WARD OFF EVIL SPIRITS SO WE HOPEFULLY ONLY CONTACT WHO WE *WANT* TO CONTACT.
WHAT DO WE DO?
I NEED TO CAST A PROTECTION SPELL.
WE HAVE TO BE AS STILL AS POSSIBLE WHILE I CAST THIS SPELL.

HINE-SI OURY IGHT-LI NO SU,
RANT-GI SU OURY HIELD-SI, EEP-KI SU AFE-SAY.

IS ANYONE ELSE, LIKE, LOW-KEY FREAKING OUT ABOUT TALKING TO SPIRITS?
HANNAH...*YOU'RE* A GHOST.

YEAH, BUT I'M NOT LIKE, A *DEAD* GHOST!

WHAT'S NEXT, ABS?
NEXT IS THE SÉANCE.
DON'T WORRY– IT'LL BE TOTALLY FINE.
OKAY, GRAB EACH OTHER'S HANDS, AND CLOSE YOUR EYES.
TAKE A FEW DEEP BREATHS, AND CLEAR YOUR MINDS.

LOOD-BI NDA-SI ONE-BA, ESPOND-RI OT YM ALL-CAY, OME-CI ORTH-FAY OM EYOND-BAY, MORRIGAN!
WHOOSH
YOU GUYS FELT THAT BREEZE TOO, RIGHT?
NOD
NOD
UHHH...MORRIGAN, ARE YOU HERE WITH US?

LOOD-BI NDA-SI ONE-BA, ESPOND-RI OT YM ALL-CAY,
OME-CI ORTH-FAY OM EYOND-BAY, MORRIGAN!

I DON'T UNDERSTAND WHY THIS ISN'T WORKING!
YOU WEREN'T SURE IT WOULD WORK IN THE FIRST PLACE...
WHY WON'T THIS WORK?!
I CAN'T EVEN PERFORM A SILLY SÉANCE RIGHT... SÉANCES ARE LIKE, WITCH 101!
HOW AM I EVER GOING TO CLOSE THE PORTAL?
YOU'RE ONE OF THE BEST STUDENTS AT SCHOOL, AND EVERYONE KNOWS HOW HARD YOU WORK. THERE ARE A MILLION REASONS WHY SUMMONING MORRIGAN MIGHT NOT BE WORKING...
THIS IS ALL MY FAULT...
IF I'D JUST LET US GET HELP IN THE FIRST PLACE, NORTH HAVEN WOULDN'T BE IN DANGER FROM A BUNCH OF RABID BUNNIES...
Grrrr...
SORRY!

WE COULD'VE TAKEN A VOTE OR INSISTED ON GETTING HELP, BUT WE DIDN'T. YOU SAID YOU COULD DO IT, AND WE BELIEVED YOU...
I *STILL* BELIEVE IN YOU, ABS. WE JUST NEED TO HURRY THINGS ALONG A LITTLE.
I BELIEVE IN YOU TOO.
YAH, ABS! WE *ALL* BELIEVE IN YOU.
THANKS, YOU GUYS...
I DON'T KNOW WHAT I WOULD DO WITHOUT YOU.
I GUESS I'LL JUST HAVE TO TRY TO FIND ANOTHER WAY TO COMMUNICATE WITH–
ABBY!

NO, WAIT-
SILAS, SHE'S COLLAPSED!
WHAT IF THE SÉANCE *DID* WORK AND MORRIGAN IS TALKING TO ABBY? WE HAVE TO GIVE HER A MINUTE.
BUT WHAT IF YOU'RE WRONG?
LET'S HOPE I'M NOT...

MOR-
MORRIGAN?
BLOOD OF MY BLOOD,
I HAVE ANSWERED YOUR SUMMONS.
HOW MAY I BE OF SERVICE?
MY MAGIC HAS BEEN ACTING DIFFERENT AND CHANGING. HOW DO I CONTROL THIS POWER?

I WANT TO MAKE EVERYTHING OKAY AGAIN. I OPENED A PORTAL, AND NOW ALL THE CHAOS BUNNIES ARE LOOSE AND DESTROYING NORTH HAVEN! EVEN THOUGH IT WAS AN ACCIDENT, I–
I DON'T WANT TO FAIL MY FRIENDS *OR* NORTH HAVEN.
IT IS TRUE THAT THE POWER IN OUR BLOOD HAS BEEN KNOWN TO BRING MADNESS WITH IT.
YOU *MUST* LEARN TO TRUST YOURSELF AND YOUR MAGIC.
BUT *HOW* DO I DO THAT?
REACH WITHIN AND FIND THE TUG OF OUR MAGIC– IT IS ALWAYS CALLING TO YOU.
THE TETHER BETWEEN US IS WEAKENING. I MUST TAKE MY LEAVE...

WAIT!
PLEASE DON'T GO YET...
I'M AFRAID I MUST.
OUR POWER–
I DON'T UNDERSTAND IT. THE SPELL I CAST WHEN I TOUCHED ELLA IN THE ALLEY... HOW I OPENED THE PORTAL...
I NEED TO KNOW HOW TO UNDO IT! PLEASE HELP ME.
YOU *DO* KNOW THE SPELL, ABIGAIL. OUR POWER PERMITS YOU TO AMPLIFY WHAT WE ARE ALREADY CAPABLE OF.
IF YOU DON'T KNOW HOW...
...MAKE SOMETHING NEW...

THAT WAS REAL, RIGHT? THAT WAS A REAL SPIRIT? YOU ALL SAW THAT TOO, RIGHT?
YEEEEEEEEP.
YOU OKAY, ABS?
YEAH, I'M OKAY. JUST TRYING TO PROCESS, Y'KNOW?
CLICK
DID ANY OF THAT...HELP?
OW...
SORRY- YEAH, SORT OF...
I STILL DON'T KNOW WHAT MORRIGAN MEANS. I DON'T KNOW HOW TO FIND THAT TUG OF MAGIC.
TINGUISH- EXI!

HAVE YOU TRIED CREATING NEW SPELLS BEFORE?
NOT REALLY...I'M STILL TRYING TO MASTER THE ONES WE'RE LEARNING IN SCHOOL.
WELL, WE'LL JUST HAVE TO KEEP TRYING TO FIGURE IT OUT.
YAH, ABS! YOU'VE *TOTALLY* GOT THIS.
I HAVE AN IDEA!
MORRIGAN SAID ABBY HAS TO LEARN TO TRUST HERSELF, RIGHT?
SHE ALREADY HAS THE POWER SHE NEEDS, SHE JUST HAS TO LEARN HOW TO TAP INTO IT.
MEET ME AT MY PLACE IN AN HOUR.
BUT WHAT ABOUT THE BUNNIES? WE NEED TO CLOSE THE PORTAL ASAP.
DID YOU SEE THEM MENTION THE CRAZY AMOUNT OF BUNNIES ON THE NEWS? THEY'RE GOING TO START INVESTIGATING IF I DON'T ACT SOON.
YEAH, BUT FIRST YOU NEED TO LEARN TO CONTROL YOUR POWERS BETTER.

TRUST ME, ABBY.
ALL WILL BE REVEALED SOON!
GOTTA GO PREPARE!
LET'S GO GRAB A DRINK DOWNSTAIRS.
WE JUST PERFORMED A SÉANCE! WE DESERVE A *SMALL* BREAK BEFORE WHATEVER GITA HAS PLANNED FOR ME.

PEST
CONTROL

ONE HOUR LATER
THE HOME OFFICES OF DRS. LYRA AND LON RILEY
AKA GITA'S PARENTS
AKA SOMEWHERE GITA ISN'T SUPPOSED TO BE...

UHHH...
SO, WHAT'S THE PLAN HERE?
WE'RE GOING TO TRY TO GET YOU IN TUNE WITH YOURSELF SO YOU CAN BETTER CHANNEL YOUR MAGIC!
LIKE, YOUR *PARENTS* ARE GOING TO HELP ME?
NO WAY, I CAN *TOTALLY* DO THIS. MY PARENTS USE THEIR PSYCHOTHERAPY ON ME AND KURT *ALL THE TIME.*
PFFT, I'M PRACTICALLY A JUNIOR PSYCHOTHERAPIST!
IT'S GOING TO BE *TOTALLY* FINE!

LET'S.
GET.
STARTED.
ABIGAIL MORGAN—MAY I CALL YOU ABBY?—WELCOME TO THIS SAFE SPACE.
EVERYTHING YOU SAY IN HERE STAYS BETWEEN YOU AND ME IN THE STRICTEST OF CONFIDENCE.
UHHH...
GREAT. ABBY, I WANT TO JUMP RIGHT INTO THINGS. YOU MENTIONED THAT YOU HAVE TROUBLE CONNECTING WITH YOURSELF—
—YOU KNOW, *INTERNALLY*— AND I HAVE SOME TOOLS THAT MAY HELP.
OKAY...
I'D LIKE FOR YOU TO TAKE A FEW DEEP BREATHS.
A BIG BREATH IN...
...AND THEN A BIG BREATH OUT.

HOW DO YOU FEEL, ABBY? DO YOU FEEL RELAXED?
HUH...I, UH, DO, ACTUALLY...
VERY GOOD. GREAT WORK SO FAR, ABBY.
I'D LIKE FOR YOU TO TRY SOMETHING ELSE NOW.
I'D LIKE FOR YOU TO SUMMON UP YOUR MAGIC–
BUT DON'T CAST A SPELL WITH IT. REACH INTO YOURSELF AND *FEEL* WHERE THAT MAGIC IS COMING FROM. CAN YOU DO THAT FOR ME?
OKAY...

DID YOU FEEL IT? COULD YOU FEEL YOUR MAGIC?!
I...DID.
I DID!
GOOD. THAT'S VERY GOOD. WELL DONE, ABBY.
NOW, WHEN MORRIGAN TOLD YOU TO FIND THE TUG OF YOUR MAGIC, WHAT DID YOU FEEL?
IT FREAKED ME OUT THAT IT COULD BE SO EASY TO CHANNEL THIS POWERFUL MAGIC IN MY BLOOD...
BUT I THINK IT'S CORRUPTED OTHER WOMEN IN OUR FAMILY OVER THE YEARS, AND...
...I'M AFRAID I'LL LOSE CONTROL.

WE'RE MAKING SOME REAL PROGRESS TODAY, ABBY.
LIKE, WHAT IF I USE MORRIGAN'S POWER AND IT CHANGES WHO I AM?!
WHAT DO YOU WANT TO USE YOUR MAGIC FOR?
WELL, WHEN I'M DONE WITH SCHOOL, I WANT TO HELP MY MOM. I WANT TO LEARN MORE ABOUT POTION-MAKING AND TAKE OVER WITCH'S BREW EVENTUALLY.
MAYBE EVEN OPEN UP A NEW CAFÉ IN ONE OF THE OTHER HAVENS.
AND HOW DO YOU THINK MORRIGAN'S POWER COULD CHANGE THAT?
...
THIS IS A SAFE SPACE, ABBY. LET IT ALL OUT!
I DON'T WANT TO END UP LIKE MY DAD!
END UP LIKE YOUR DAD HOW?
HE *LEFT* US. HE GAVE UP ON US...I DON'T WANT TO LOSE MY FAMILY. NOT EVER.

AHHHH...*NOW* WE'RE REALLY GETTING SOMEWHERE. GOOD, ABBY.
DO YOU FEEL YOUR MOM HOLDS RESENTMENT TOWARD YOUR FATHER?
NO...
SHE SAYS SHE UNDERSTANDS WHY HE HAD TO GO...WHY HE RETURNED TO THE WILDS TO BECOME A HIGH PRIEST. SHE SAYS WE ALL NEED A CALLING AND IT DIDN'T CHANGE HIS LOVE FOR US...
BUT HOW COULD HE JUST *LEAVE* US? HOW COULD YOU CHANGE *THAT* MUCH AND SUDDENLY WANT SOMETHING COMPLETELY DIFFERENT? WHAT IF MY POWER FROM MORRIGAN CHANGES *ME*?
YOU THINK YOU'LL JUST *CHANGE* AND WANT TO LEAVE YOUR FAMILY IF YOU USE MORRIGAN'S POWER?
I LOVE MY FAMILY MORE THAN ANYTHING. I COULD NEVER TURN MY BACK ON THEM...OR YOU...I MEAN, MY FRIENDS!
STOP FOR A SECOND...
LET YOURSELF FEEL THAT PASSION FOR EVERYONE YOU LOVE.
HOLD ON TO THAT FEELING YOU HAVE RIGHT NOW. *THAT* IS YOUR TETHER TO THE TRUE ABBY. IF YOU FEEL LOST, REMEMBER THAT.

WOW... THAT'S HEAVY...
BUT GOOD.
I TOLD YOU! ALL THESE YEARS OF LIVING WITH PSYCHOTHERAPIST PARENTS HAS FINALLY PAID OFF!
THANKS, GITA.
WHAT WERE YOU WRITING ON THAT PAD?
YOU HAD ME SO PARANOID ABOUT WHAT MIGHT BE WRONG WITH ME, AND YOU'VE JUST BEEN *DOODLING*?!
YOU'RE REALLY GOOD...
THANKS!
...IF YOU JUST STEP IN HERE, WE CAN GET STARTED ON TODAY'S SESS–

GITA!
YOU KNOW YOU'RE NOT SUPPOSED TO BE IN HERE...

UH, HI, MOM! WE WERE, UH, JUST LEAVING!
BYE, MOM!
HI, MRS. RILEY! BYE, MRS. RILEY!

YOUR MOM DID *NOT* LOOK HAPPY TO SEE US!
I AM *DEFINITELY* GOING TO HEAR ABOUT THAT LATER, BUT IT'S OKAY. IT WAS WORTH IT!
WE SHOULD GO TO MY PLACE. I WANT TO TRY CLOSING THE PORTAL.
I THINK I'M READY.
I'M PROUD OF YOU.
THANKS, GITA.
LET'S TEXT HANNAH AND SILAS AND HAVE THEM MEET US. WE'RE ALL IN THIS TOGETHER.
LET'S DO THIS!

WE SHOULD PROBABLY GET TO MY PLACE QUICKLY...
AGREED.
WAAAAAAIT!
WAAAHAAH!

SORRY SORRY SORRY! EVERYTHING'S FINE...I WAS JUST THINKING WE SHOULD BE PREPARED.
YOU KNOW, JUST IN CASE WE RUN INTO ANY OF THE BUNNIES!
HMM, GOOD POINT...
BUT WHAT SHOULD WE USE?
I HAVE ANOTHER IDEA!

MOMENTS LATER...
THOSE BUNNIES BETTER NOT MESS WITH US!
YEAAAAAH!
HIYAAAAAAAAAAAAAAAH–
WATCH OUT, CHAOS!
... BUNNIES ...

GRRRRRRRR
RAAAAAAAaH

WAAAAAAAH!
RUN, RUN, RUN!

REEZE-FI NI RACKS-TAE!
??
??
sniff
sniff
sniff
WITCH'S BREW

huff
huff
huff
HEY, GITA, YOU DEAD, GIRL?
YAH, GIRL...

ABBY'S APARTMENT
THE LIVING ROOM
CLICK
-YOU CAN SEE AROUND ME, NORTH HAVEN IS IN *UTTER CHAOS* AS PEST CONTROL AND AUTHORITIES SCRAMBLE TO GET THIS SUDDEN INFESTATION UNDER CONTROL AND DISCOVER THE CAUSE.
AUTHORITIES ARE ADVISING CITIZENS TO STAY INDOORS AND ARE URGED TO NOT TAKE MATTERS INTO THEIR OWN HANDS-
WELL, I THINK *THAT* SHIP HAS SAILED...

GARY, WHAT ARE YOU DOING? MOVE THE CAMERA BACK–
WAAAAAAAAAGHHHHHHH!
GARY– HEEEEEEEEEEELP!
THIS HAS BEEN AN ON-THE-STREETS REPORT. FOR NHNS-TV, I AM CHUCK MARKOVICH. UNTIL NEXT TIME–
OH DEAR GODS, SEND HEEEEEELP!

CLICK
UMMM...
WE SHOULD PROBABLY
GET THAT PORTAL
CLOSED.
NOD
NOD
NOD
NOD
NORTH HAVEN IS IN REALLY ROUGH
SHAPE—THE CHAOS BUNNIES ARE
TEARING EVERYTHING APART. AND
THEY'RE DEFINITELY GOING TO DETECT
THE PORTAL SOON.
I SHOULD'VE ASKED FOR
HELP RIGHT AWAY—I'M SORRY
FOR LETTING THINGS GET
THIS BAD...
BUT I REALLY THINK
I CAN FIX IT NOW,
THANKS TO GITA.

CAN WE PLEASE FOCUS?!
SNAP
SNAP
HEYA!
UH, ELLA, WE'RE ABOUT TO TRY A SPELL I HAVEN'T TRIED BEFORE–
DO YOU THINK YOU CAN MAAAAAAYBE GO TO YOUR ROOM FOR A BIT?
UGH, FIIIIIIINE...

WHUMP!

AS I WAS SAYING–
WHUMP
LET'S TRY THAT AGAIN.
AS I WAS SAYING–
WHUMP
WHUMP
WHUMP
ELLAAAAAAAAA!!!

ELLA, SO HELP ME...
STOP SLAMMING YOUR DOOR.
YOU NEVER LET ME DO ANYTHING FUN!
I'M JUST TRYING TO PROTECT YOU–I DON'T KNOW HOW THIS WILL GO.
I CAN TAKE CARE OF MYSELF!
YOU'RE JUST A KID.
AM NOT!
YES. YOU. ARE.
UGHHHHH.
UGHHHHHHH RIGHT BACK.
...
YOU CAN HANG OUT WITH US AFTERWARD ...OKAY?
REALLY?
...
YOU PROMISE?
YES, I PROMISE!
OKAY.
OKAY!
LOVE YOU...
LOVE YOU TOO, ELLA...

SIBLINGS, AMIRITE?!
I HAD A WHOLE SPEECH PLANNED OUT, BUT LET'S JUST CUT TO THE CHASE–
CLICK
GITA HELPED ME REACH WITHIN MYSELF AND FIGURE OUT THE SOURCE OF MY MAGIC AND BLAH BLAH BLAH BLAH...
AND I THINK I'M READY.
LET'S GET OUT TO THE PORTAL AND CLOSE IT!

ALL RIIIIIIIGHT, IT'S TIME TO GET DOWN TO BUSINESS.
THESE BUNNIES HAVE INFESTED THE *WRONG TOWN.*
IT'S OUR JOB TO SEND 'EM BACK TO THEIR OWN DIMENSION, AND *MAKE 'EM SORRY!*

YOU LOT ARE ALL THAT'S STANDING BETWEEN OUR WORLD AND ITS TOTAL DESTRUCTION BY BUNNY.
IT'S TIME TO GO BACK DOWN TO THAT ALLEY.
AND IT'S TIME TO CLOSE THAT PORTAL.
WE DO THIS NOT JUST FOR US, BUT FOR THE ENTIRE TOWN OF NORTH HAVEN, ALL OF THE WILDS, THE OTHER HAVENS, AND OUR *WORLD.*
TONIGHT, WE ARE CANCELING THE A-HOP-CALYPSE!

OFFICER MORGAN, YOUR MISSION IS TO USE YOUR SUPER MAGIC TO CLOSE THE PORTAL.
OFFICERS RILEY AND SWAYZE–
HIYA!
SWAYZE, SPEAK ONLY WHEN SPOKEN TO. IS THAT CLEAR?
UHH... YES?
YES, SIR!

I THINK YOU MIGHT BE TAKING THIS A BIT TOO SERIOUSLY...

OFFICERS, YOU WILL BE OUR DEFENSE. I'LL NEED YOU TO SUIT UP AND PREPARE YOURSELVES.

AND YOU-
UHHHH, ABS...
ELLA, I TOLD YOU TO HANG OUT IN YOUR ROOM!
AND I *DID*, BUT I WANT TO HANG OUT WITH *YOU* NOW. IT'S BORING IN THERE...
Sigh
ELLA, PLEASE. I NEED YOU TO SIT THIS ONE OUT. FOR ME.
CAN YOU TRUST ME ON THIS?
UGH...
FINE... OOOO-KAY...

SORRY!
IT'S ALL RIGHT, CADET.
FALL IN LINE AND LET'S CARRY ON...
GITA. HANNAH. IT'S TIME. SUIT UP AND PREPARE FOR BATTLE...

THE ALLEY

OKAY, ABBY...
YOU CAN DO
THIS.

OKAY... HERE GOES...
ISPEL-DE... UHHH... PORTAL.

DOES ANYTHING SEEM DIFFERENT TO YOU?
NO...
SORRY, ABS.
MAYBE TRY A PROTECTION SPELL? THAT WORKED LAST TIME, SO START WITH THAT!

GOOD IDEA!
HINE-SI OURY IGHT-LI NO SU,
RANT-GI SU OURY HIELD-SI, EEP-KI SU AFE-SAY.

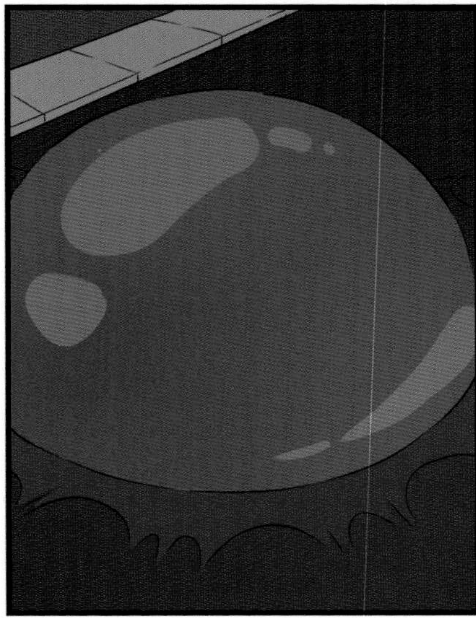

WAIT!

I'LL BE RIGHT BY YOUR SIDE.

SWIPE
AHEM...
MISSING THIS?
OH! WHOOPS...
I'LL JUST STAND HERE...
BUT I SUPPORT YOU TOO!

YOU CAN DO THIS, ABS.
REMEMBER— WE'RE HERE FOR YOU.
YOU SHOULD STAND BACK WITH HANNAH IN CASE ANYTHING GOES WRONG...
NAH, YOU'VE GOT THIS.

DISPEL!

WHOOSH
AAAABBBBBBBY...
WHOOSH
WHAT'S GOING ON? SHOULDN'T ABBY'S PROTECTION SPELL BE, YOU KNOW, *PROTECTING* US?
I DON'T KNOW...
NOTHING SHOULD BE ABLE TO GET IN!

WE'LL DEAL WITH WHATEVER IT IS...
WE'VE GOT THIS.
WHOOSH
HOW FOOLISH THEY LOOK...
WHOOSH
WHOOSH
WHAP

WHAT THE–
HA
HA
HA
HA
HA
HA
HA
HA

HELLO AGAIN, ABBY...
YOU'RE SO PATHETIC...
CAN'T GET YOUR MAGIC UNDER CONTROL...
WEAK, POWERLESS...
STOP IT!
STOP IT?
STOP IT OR *WHAT?*
WHAT ARE *YOU* GOING TO DO ABOUT IT?

WHAT ARE THE CHAOS BUNNIES DOING?!
I-I THINK THEY CAN SENSE THAT WE'RE DOING SOMETHING TO THE PORTAL.
WHUMP!
I'M HERE TO HELP!

ELLA! COME HERE!
OH MY GOSH, GET OVER HERE!
HURRY UP!
I SHOULD'VE LISTENED TO ABBY...

WAAAAAH!

WHAT IS A LITTLE WITCH LIKE *YOU* GOING TO DO?
YOU *COULD* DO SOMETHING ABOUT IT...
IF YOU EMBRACED THE *TRUE* POWER WITHIN YOU...
IF YOU JUST LET IT LOOSE...
BANG
BANG
BANG

ARE YOU OKAY?
LEAVE HER ALONE!
DOES THE WOLF GIRL THINK SHE CAN STOP *ME*?
SHE HAS NO POWER HERE...

LEAVE. HER. ALONE.
Bmp
Bmp
Bmp
OHHHHH, LOOKS LIKE THE WOLF GIRL HAS A CRUSH ON YOU...
DO YOU NEED YOUR GIRLFRIEND TO SAVE YOU?
LEAVE ME ALONE.
I KNOW WHO I AM...
I AM ABBY MORGAN.
AND I AM POWERFUL.
I DON'T NEED YOU...

HA HA, YOU WILL NEVER BE-
NO.
I'M DONE LISTENING TO YOU.
NOW *YOU* LISTEN TO *ME*...
YOU ARE GOING TO *LEAVE ME ALONE.*
YOU ARE GOING TO LEAVE *US* ALONE.
THAT'S NOT HOW THIS WOR-
LEAVE ME ALONE!

WE SHOULD GET TO COVER OVER THERE.

I DON'T UNDERSTAND WHY IT'S NOT CLOSING ALL THE WAY...
ABBY, THE BUNNY.
YEAH, THERE WERE *LOTS* OF BUNNIES...
NO, ABBY... *THE* BUNNY.
THE BUNNY IN YOUR ROOM!

BE RIGHT BACK...
Grrrrrr

OKAY, OKAY...
!!!

IS IT OVER?

I CAN'T FEEL IT...
CAN'T FEEL WHAT, ABS?
THE PORTAL!
IT'S GONE! WE CLOSED IT!
NO, *YOU* CLOSED IT.
YOU DID IT!

CRASH!!
OH NO–
THE PORTAL MUST'VE CLOSED WITHOUT ONE OF THE BUNNIES!
LET'S CHECK IT OUT...
tkt
tkt
tkt
tkt
tkt

!!
AHA HA HA HA HA AHA AHA AHA HA AHA
OH, THANK GOODNESS...
WE'VE HAD A LONG DAY...
I THINK IT'S TIME WE HEAD INSIDE FOR A CELEBRATORY DRINK ON THE HOUSE.
UGH YESSSSSSSSSS... I WOULD LOOOOVE A HOT CHOCOLATE.
NOD
NOD
NOD
NOD
ME TOO!

EPILOGUE
THAT LOOKS REALLY GOOD, LOVE!
MAKE SURE TO WRITE THAT SPELL DOWN IN YOUR BOOK.
THANKS!
Abby Morgan's Book of Homecrafted Spells

WELL, WHADDAYA THINK?
IT'S SO GOOD, ABS!
I'M REALLY HAPPY WITH HOW THIS ONE TURNED OUT!
MY MOM THINKS THEY'RE GOOD ENOUGH TO ADD TO THE MENU SOON.
I HATE TO BE A PARTY POOPER, BUT I HAVE TO GO SOON...
AWWW, WHAT?
YOU'LL MISS THE COMMUNITY CLEANUP DAY!
I KNOW, BUT, UH-

MY PARENTS GOT A SPECIAL TRAVEL VISA FOR ME SO I COULD GO BACK TO MY HOME DIMENSION. IT WAS A SURPRISE GIFT!
I LEAVE IN A COUPLE HOURS THROUGH A *LEGAL* AUTHORIZED PORTAL.
WHAT? NO WAY!
THAT'S SO COOL!
YOUR GRANDMA WILL BE SO EXCITED TO SEE YOU!
I HAVE A *MILLION* QUESTIONS THAT I WANT TO ASK AND A LIST OF EVERYTHING I WANT TO SEE!
I'M GONNA NEED A NEW SCRAPBOOK...
OKAY. TIME TO GO...

WE'RE GONNA MISS YOU, HANNAH!
HUG!
I'M NOT GOING *FOREVER*. JUST FOR A FEW WEEKS!
I'LL BE BACK BEFORE YOU KNOW IT. JUST IN TIME FOR THE BEGINNING OF SCHOOL.
NO OPENING ANY PORTALS TO DIMENSIONS WITH DESTRUCTIVE ANIMALS WHILE I'M GONE!
WE'LL DO OUR BEST!
TAKE LOTS OF PHOTOS!
AND DON'T FORGET TO SEND US IDMAIL!*
*IDMAIL = INTERDIMENSIONAL DIGITAL MAIL—LIKE EMAIL BUT IT CAN TRAVEL THROUGH DIMENSIONS!
WE SHOULD GET GOING.
THE CLEANUP STARTS SOON, AND I DON'T WANT TO BE LATE.

UH, HEY, ABS, CAN I TALK TO YOU A SEC?
I GUESS I'LL WAIT FOR YOU OUTSIDE...
BUT I DO **NOT** WANT TO BE LATE!
THANKS, SI...
IS EVERYTHING OKAY?
OH! YEAH, EVERYTHING IS FINE! I, UH-
I JUST WANTED TO TALK TO YOU-
ABOUT-

I-
I WANTED TO ASK IF-
WHAT'S THAT SHOW YOU'RE ALWAYS TALKING ABOUT... SOMETHING *RIDERS*?
CRYSTAL RIDERS?
YEAH! IT'S ON TONIGHT, RIGHT?
YAH...
I WAS WONDERING IF YOU MIGHT WANT TO WATCH IT WITH ME.
WITH YOU?
WITH, UH, *JUST* ME...
WAIT-
I THOUGHT YOU DIDN'T KNOW ANYTHING ABOUT *CRYSTAL RIDERS*?
I KNOW IT'S YOUR FAVORITE...
I'VE BEEN TRYING TO GET CAUGHT UP-
AND I'VE BEEN READING THE WICCI PAGES ON THE SHOW...
I WAS THINKING MAYBE YOU COULD FILL ME IN ON EVERYTHING ELSE.

I CAN'T BELIEVE YOU WANT TO WATCH *CRYSTAL RIDERS!*
I'M *SO* EXCITED.
WE'LL TALK BEFORE THE SHOW STARTS AND FIGURE OUT HOW MUCH YOU KNOW AND–
I'M JUST HAPPY THAT YOU WANT TO WATCH IT.
YOU KNOW, WITH ME.
ME TOO.
ARE YOU TWO **COMING** OR WHAT?!
WE'RE COMING, WE'RE COMING...

NORTH HAVEN PARK
COMMUNITY CLEANUP DAY

NORTH HAVEN COMMUNITY CLEANUP DAY
NORTH HAVEN COMMUNITY CLEANUP DAY
NORTH HAVEN COMMUNITY CLEANUP DAY

NORTH
HAVEN
COMMUNITY
CLEANUP
DAY

HERE'S A VOUCHER FOR A FREE DRINK AT WITCH'S BREW.
THANK YOU FOR YOUR HARD WORK!
NORTH HAVEN COMMUNITY CLEANUP DAY
NORTH HAVEN COMMUNITY CLEANUP DAY

NORTH HAVEN COMMUNITY CLEANUP DAY
NORTH HAVEN COMMUNITY CLEANUP DAY
NORTH HAVEN COMMUNITY CLEANUP DAY

YOU DID REALLY GOOD TODAY.
NORTH HAVEN COMMUNITY CLEANUP DAY
WE DID REALLY GOOD TODAY.
THIS ALL HAPPENED BECAUSE OF ME...
BUT WE FIXED IT!
YEAH! AND YOU'RE A BETTER WITCH BECAUSE OF IT.
NORTH HAVEN
I'M GOING TO KEEP PRACTICING, AND I'VE BEEN MEDITATING EVERY NIGHT TO BETTER BE IN TOUCH WITH MY POWERS!
COME WITH ME. I WANT TO SHOW YOU SOMETHING.
WOW, SILAS. THIS IS BEAUTIFUL!
IT'S MY FAVORITE PLACE IN THE WHOLE WORLD...

!
SNIFF
SNIFF
YOU OKAY?
I AM NOW.

WiTCH'S BREW CAFÉ VLOG

NORTHERN EVERGREEN MATCHA LATTE

1

TO START, YOU'RE GOING TO WANT TO PUT ALL THE WATER INTO A SMALL POT. PUT IT ON THE STOVE AND BRING THE WATER TO A BOIL—YOU CAN ASK A PARENT TO HELP YOU!

ONCE IT STARTS TO BOIL, YOU WANT TO ADD YOUR MATCHA AND MIX IT TOGETHER. THEN REMOVE THE POT FROM THE STOVE.